The
moon in my
room

For Helene

The moon in my room

by Uri Shulevitz

A Sunburst Book
Farrar Straus Giroux

Distributed in Canada by Douglas & McIntyre Ltd.
Printed and bound in China
First published by Harper & Row, 1963
First Sunburst edition, 2003
10 9 8 7 6 5 4 3 2 1

Library of Congress Cataloging-in-Publication Data
Shulevitz, Uri, 1935–
    The moon in my room / by Uri Shulevitz.— 1st Sunburst ed.
        p.   cm.
    "A Sunburst book."
    Summary: In his room, a young boy has his own sun, moon, stars, flowers,
train, and more, but his world is incomplete until he finds his dear bear.
    ISBN 0-374-45314-4 (pbk.)
    [1. Teddy bears—Fiction.]   I. Title.

PZ7.S5594 Mo 2003
[E]—dc21
                                        2002027895

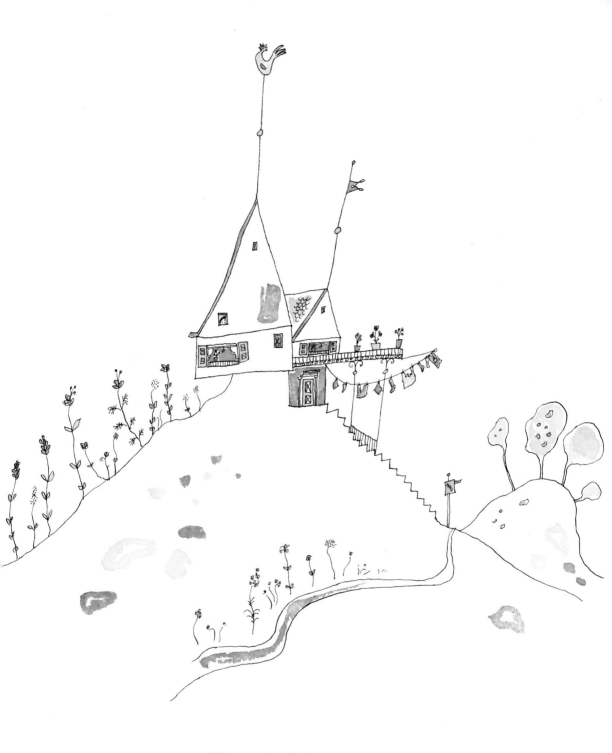

This is the little house.

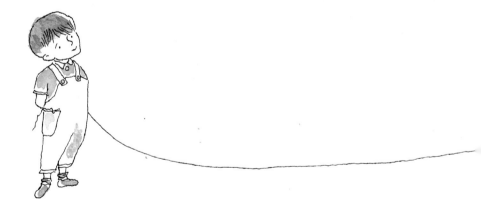

This is the little boy.

This is his little room.
In his little room there is a whole world.

He has his private sun,

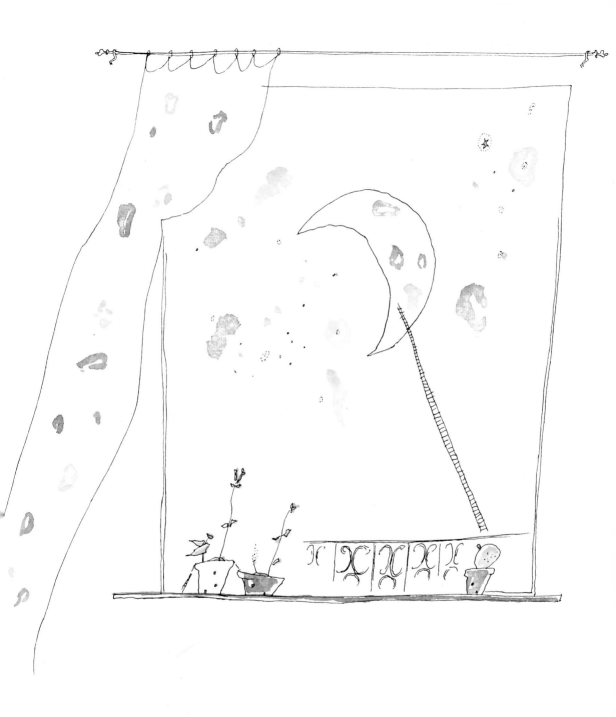

a private moon all for himself,

and private stars,

a garden with trees and flowers,

mountains and valleys,

and many friends:

Toy Soldier,

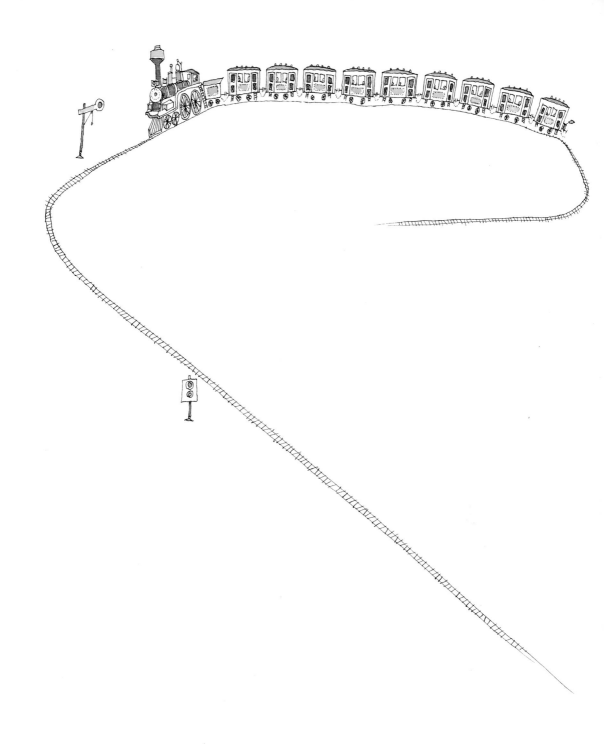

Train,

Cannon,

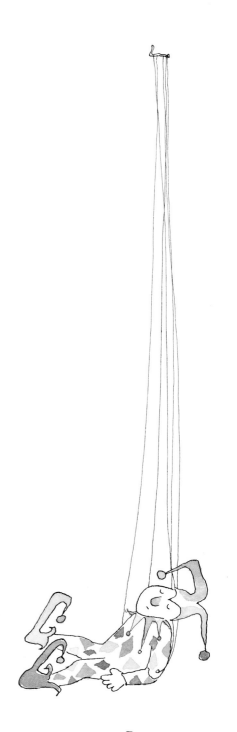

Puppet,

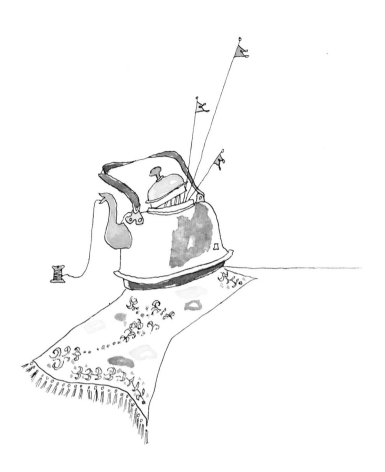

Old Pot . . .
But where is Prince Bear?

Maybe in his little castle? No.

In the little garden, perhaps? No.

Under the table? No.

On the closet? No.

"Where can he be? I will miss him so much!

Where are you, Prince Bear?
Please come back!"

"Here I am," said Prince Bear
from under the bed.

"Why did you leave me?" asked the boy.

"Because you forgot me and stopped
  playing with me."

"Oh, no! I missed you," said the little boy,
and he hugged Prince Bear.

"I have a crown for you.
From now on you will be king.

I have the whole world in my room.
You will have part of my private moon

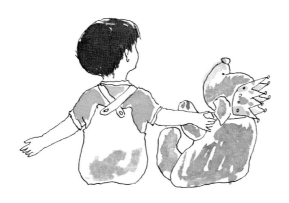

and my private stars.

And we will always be friends.
Good night, Bear."
"Good night . . ."